This book belongs to

. . . . . . . . . . . . . . . . . . . . . . . . . . . . . . . . .

*To the memory of Florrie.*
*And for Paul, with love and thanks,*
*for believing and being there.*

EGMONT

*We bring stories to life*

Our story began over a century ago, when seventeen-year-old Egmont Harald Petersen found a coin in the street.
He was on his way to buy a flyswatter, a small hand-operated printing machine that he then set up in his tiny apartment.

The coin brought him such good luck that today Egmont has offices in over 30 countries around the world.
And that lucky coin is still kept at the company's head offices in Denmark.

First published in Great Britain, 1998
by Methuen Children's Books as *Little Robin Red Vest*
Published in this edition as *Little Robin's Christmas* in Great Britain 2013
by Egmont UK Limited, The Yellow Building
1 Nicholas Road, London W11 4AN

www.egmont.co.uk


A CIP catalogue record is available from the British Library

ISBN 978 1 4052 6855 4

# Little Robin's Christmas

Jan Fearnley

EGMONT

It was the week before Christmas and Little Robin was getting very excited. He washed and ironed seven warm vests for the frosty days ahead.

He put on his white vest
and set out to skate on the pond.
On the way, he met Frog.
"I'm so cold!" said Frog. "Can you help?"

Little Robin gave Frog his white vest.
“I’ve still got six vests left,” he thought,
as Frog hopped off happily.

Six days before Christmas, Little Robin
put on his green vest and dashed out
to play in the snow.
Down the path came Hedgehog.
"I'm freezing!" he said.

Little Robin gave Hedgehog his green vest.
"I've still got five vests left," he thought,
waving goodbye to his prickly friend.

Five days before Christmas, Little Robin put on
his pink vest, and went to look for worms.

He hadn't gone far when Mole appeared.
"Brrrrrrr! The ground's too hard to dig,
and I'm chilly!" he complained.

So Little Robin gave his pink vest to Mole.
It was a bit tight, but Mole didn't mind.
He was nice and warm.
"Four vests left," thought Little Robin.

Four days before Christmas, Little Robin put on his yellow vest and flew up to sit in the tall oak tree where he met Squirrel.

"I'm so cold I can't sleep!" Squirrel grumbled.

Little Robin handed over his yellow vest.
"Only three vests left now," he thought,
as Squirrel dozed off.

Three days before Christmas,
Little Robin put on his blue vest.

He was swooping
down through the clouds
when he saw Rabbit on the hill.
"I'm so cold my teeth are
chattering!" shivered Rabbit.

Little Robin gave Rabbit his blue vest.
"Well, I've still got two left," he said to himself,
as Rabbit went cheerfully on his way.
Two days before Christmas, Little Robin put on
his purple vest and skipped along the river bank.

Next to the river stood Otter with
her baby. She was very unhappy.
"My baby is poorly!" she said.

Little Robin's purple vest was just right for
Baby Otter, and made him feel much better.
"Oh dear, I've only one vest left," thought Little Robin.

On the day before Christmas, Little Robin put on his very last vest, a warm, orange one. He'd been walking and whistling to himself for some time when he met a little mouse, shivering in the garden.

Little Robin felt so sorry for her that he
took off his last woolly vest and pulled
it over her chilly little ears.

Now it was late on Christmas Eve, the snow was falling and poor Little Robin had nothing warm to wear. There was nobody around to help him, and it was a long way home. He fluffed up his feathers as best he could and huddled miserably on a snowy roof.

Soon he fell fast asleep.
Not even the sleigh bells
woke him. Or the crunch
of snow under two heavy,
black boots.

Large hands scooped
Little Robin up and
tucked him into a soft
white beard.
“You had better come
with me, my lad!” chuckled
a gruff, jolly voice.

“This is the generous little fellow I told you about,”
the man said to his wife.
“He must have a very special present then,” she replied.

And with Little Robin snug and cosy in her lap,
the lady set to work . . . She pulled a thread from a big,
bright red coat, and with it she knitted a tiny vest.
It was a perfect fit for a little bird.

"I'm very proud of you," said the man, with a smile. "You gave away all your warm clothes to help other people. You are full of the spirit of Christmas.

Now it's time for your present. This vest is very, very special. It will keep you warm forever, and when other people see you, it will make them feel warm too."

It was time to go, back across the skies as the sun rose to kiss the land. Little Robin was very happy. His chest glowed as red as a reindeer's nose.

Soon Little Robin was home. “Merry Christmas!”
cried the man as he flew off.
“Goodbye, and thank you!” Little Robin shouted back.

It was Christmas morning. Boys and girls
everywhere were opening their presents.
Little Robin flew to the highest branch, proudly
wearing his new red vest, and sang out sweetly
to wish everyone a "Merry Christmas!"